All Aboard to FAIRVILLE
and other stories

by Rachel Stein
Illustrated by Racheli David

ISRAEL BOOKSHOP
Publications

All Aboard to FAIRVILLE

and other stories

by Rachel Stein

Illustrated by Racheli David

Copyright © 2017 by Israel Bookshop Publications

ISBN 978-1-60091-530-7

Distributed by:
Israel Bookshop Publications
501 Prospect Street
Lakewood, NJ 08701
Tel: (732) 901-3009 / Fax: (732) 901-4012
www.israelbookshoppublications.com
info@israelbookshoppublications.com

Printed in the United States of America

Distributed in Israel by:
Shanky's
Petach Tikva 16
Jerusalem
972-2-538-6936

Distributed in Europe by:
Lehmanns
Unit E Viking Industrial Park
Rolling Mill Road,
Jarrow, Tyne & Wear NE32 3DP
44-191-430-0333

Distributed in Australia by:
Gold's Book and Gift Company
3-13 William Street
Balaclava 3183
613-9527-8775

Distributed in South Africa by:
Kollel Bookshop
Northfield Centre
17 Northfield Avenue
Glenhazel 2192
27-11-440-6679

Table of Contents

Dear Readers

Dear Readers,

I'd like to invite you to join me on a trip to meet kids just like you. I hope you enjoy meeting them as I enjoyed writing about them. But before we go, here's some food for thought to pack in your carry-on.

Three little words...

Three giant words...

Well, you must be wondering, which is it? Little or big? Before I tell you, close your eyes for a moment and see if this sounds familiar:

"He got a bigger piece than me!"

"She got a higher grade, and I worked so hard!"

"Why did she win first place? I should have won!"

And now, the call of those famous words, small in the amount of letters, but carrying a BIG message: "IT'S NOT FAIR!"

Have you ever said or felt these words? If your answer is yes, you're not alone—most of us have, at some time or another. Because our eyes show us that she's prettier, he's smarter, she's wealthy, he's Mr. Popular—and it just doesn't seem, well, fair.

When was the last time you went to the zoo? Did you ever notice a turtle feeling jealous of the cheetah, or a zebra resenting a lion?

You're probably shaking your head with the hint of a smile. Of course the animals don't envy each other! Ever wonder why?

Hashem gave each animal a job. In order to do that job, each creature has exactly what it needs. So the giraffe doesn't wish it could fly, and the lion doesn't want to swim like a dolphin, as fun as it may look.

And it's the same for us. If Chavie has a beautiful voice, and Dovid is brilliant, those are the gifts they need to reach their goals in this world. We have other gifts, whatever we need to reach our goals.

So we have a choice. We can stamp our feet and grumble, "It's not fair!" when we see someone who has something very special. Or we can tilt our chins, smile, and thank Hashem for giving us the perfect tools to help us do exactly what we're supposed to do!

So come on, kids! Fasten your seatbelts, and here's wishing you a pleasant trip as you go *All Aboard to Fairville!*

Warmly,

Rachel Stein

Acknowledgments

With love and appreciation to:

My amazing husband, children, and grandchildren—thank you for being the absolute best ever!

My awesome sister and brother-in-law, my dear mother-in-law, and my wonderful Aunt Betty!

My thanks to the wonderful staff at Israel Bookshop. In particular, thank you to Mrs. M. Gendelman for her magical editing pen; to Mrs. K. Nisenbaum and Mrs. R. Gemal for their meticulous proofreading; and Mrs. R. David for her delightful illustrations.

An Elephant-Sized Lesson

One beautiful Sunday morning, when a perfectly blue sky hung overhead, Avrami woke up with a grin as bright as the sun. Today was the day their family was going to the zoo, his favorite outing. From the time his mother had announced plans for the trip, the days seemed to pass as slowly as a turtle plodding along a winding trail.

If there was one place Avrami loved, it was the Lakeshore Zoo. One of the best parts about the zoo was the huge cages the animals lived in. Lakeshore tried to recreate the animals' natural habitats, so the animals had lots of space to romp with plants and water similar to their homes in the wild.

Avrami hoped they would get to see all the animals today—from the funny monkeys to the jumping kangaroos. Maybe they could even stay for some of the animal shows.

With a whispered *Modeh Ani* and a flurried *negel vasser* washing, Avrami was up and dressed before his little brother and sister even opened their eyes.

"Get up, sleepy heads," he crowed. "Did you forget? Today we're going to the zoo!"

Sori and Moishe blinked and sat upright.

"Yay!" they said together, jumping out of bed and dashing to the kitchen for breakfast.

Delicious pancakes sizzled on the stove, and Mommy flipped a few onto a plate and passed it to Moishe.

"Hey, why does he get first?" Avrami complained, grabbing Moishe's plate away and putting it in front of his own seat.

"Mommy!" Moishe cried. "Avrami took my pancakes!"

Before Mommy could say a word, the boys began to play tug-of-war with the plate. Suddenly, the plate slipped out of their hands. Wide-eyed, the children watched as the whole plate, with its stack of pancakes dripping maple syrup, plopped down and landed straight on Sori's lap.

"Now look what you did!" Avrami pointed to the mess, his eyes narrowed angrily. "Maybe we should leave you at the zoo with the animals."

"Avrami!" Mommy warned, reaching for the paper towels and handing them to both boys.

"It's his fault," Avrami grumbled as he swiped at the sticky mess. "If he had let me take first, this never would have happened. I'm older, and I should get first."

"It's your fault!" Moishe insisted, blinking back tears.

"How about finishing breakfast and *davening*?" Mommy suggested, trying to change the subject. "The faster everyone gets ready, the sooner we'll be able to go."

Avrami quickly finished his portion and *davened*. Then he began hopping from one foot to the other, looking at the clock every five minutes.

"We still have a little while," Mommy told him. "Can you go find a friend until we're ready to leave?"

Just then the doorbell rang, and Avrami rushed to answer it.

"Hi, Naftali," he greeted his friend eagerly, opening the door wide. "Wanna play a game?"

"Sure," Naftali agreed, following Avrami to the playroom.

"You can go first," Avrami said once the game was set up.

Moishe sauntered in. "Can I play winner?" he asked.

"No," Avrami said shortly. "Leave us alone."

With his shoulders slumped, Moishe shuffled out of the room.

"Avrami, move your red piece," Sori suggested, coming close and trying to help.

"Can't we play in peace?" Avrami snapped. "Go away!"

Sniffling, Sori walked away from the game and went to play with her dolls.

Close to an hour later, the game wound down.

"Good game," Avrami announced. "You won."

"Avrami, Moishe, Sori, time to go!" Mommy called.

"Thanks for coming," Avrami said, walking Naftali to the door. "We're off to the zoo now. Maybe we can play again later, okay?"

"Sure," Naftali said. "See you."

"You know, I wish you were as nice to us as you are to your friends," Moishe muttered to Avrami as they left the house.

"Maybe if you weren't so annoying—" Avrami began, but Mommy interrupted him.

"Avrami, Moishe, please, let's not argue. Everyone, into the minivan!"

The kids strapped themselves in, and Mommy

pulled out of the driveway. At last they were on their way to the zoo!

Once they bought their tickets and walked through the gates, Avrami wasn't disappointed. To his delight, the monkeys performed acrobatics, swinging from branch to branch by their arms and tails and making him laugh out loud. Lions and tigers roared, and a shiver passed through him as he watched and listened. The pandas were so cute, rolling over and playing, looking like big stuffed animals.

"Look at the elephants!" Mommy said, motioning to the next exhibit. "A whole family of them, two parents and two babies. Isn't that cute?"

They all went over to the exhibit to look. As they watched, one of the baby elephants waddled around, and then suddenly tripped and fell, lying helplessly on its side. Flailing its arms and legs, the baby elephant couldn't seem to get itself back up again.

"Poor thing!" Avrami gasped. "Who will help him?"

Tatty and Mommy Elephant rushed over to the rescue. They nudged the baby elephant with their trunks and giant feet, but the baby elephant was still stuck on its side. Then Brother Elephant trundled forward. Using his trunk, he worked together with his parents to push the helpless little elephant back into a standing position. Just when it looked like the baby was finally upright, its feet slid out from underneath, and it fell back down.

"Oh, no!" Avrami, Moishe, and Sori cried out together, putting their hands over their mouths.

"Come on," Avrami urged the elephants, "don't give up! This is your son, this is your brother! Try again!"

The elephants seemed determined, even without Avrami's urging. They didn't leave the baby for a second. They heaved, tugged, pushed, and pulled. Two more times the little elephant's feet slid out

from under it, and it toppled again, until finally, success! With the combined efforts of all three elephants, the little elephant struggled and stood solidly upright, flicking its tail.

Mrs. Elephant trumpeted loudly. Avrami was sure she was saying, "*Baruch Hashem!*"

"Yay!" the Cohens cheered happily, letting out a whoosh of relief.

"What a show!" Moishe whistled as they finally moved on, heading down the path.

"Yeah," Sori agreed. "That was neat."

Avrami was strangely quiet, thinking about what he had seen.

"Okay," Mommy said, glancing at the map. "We can either go to a reptile show or see the bears. What'll it be?"

Avrami wanted to see the bears first. He loved to watch the big polar bears swim. "Bears!" he said.

"Reptile show!" Moishe and Sori called out at the same time.

Avrami paused for a moment. Then he said, "Okay, let's go to the reptile show first. We can see the bears later."

Mommy gazed at Avrami in surprise and praised him. "How nice of you, Avrami!"

Avrami pictured the family of elephants working together to help their little guy. "It's no big deal," he said with a shrug. "It's just what siblings do for each other."

With a grin, he turned to Moishe and Sori. "Come on, guys! Hurry up! We want to get good seats."

Holding hands, Avrami, Moishe, and Sori ran toward the reptile arena together. Mommy's smile matched Avrami's from early that morning, bright as the afternoon sun.

The Real WinneR

"Mommy, I won the class spelling bee!" Bracha Ora blew into the house breathlessly with her news, two bright pink spots coloring her cheeks, and her gray eyes sparkling.

"Mazel tov, honey!" Mommy replied, giving her a warm smile. "I'm really proud of you!"

"Yeah," Bracha Ora said dreamily. "Esther Leah and I were the only two girls left, and then I knew the last answer and she didn't. It was amazing!"

"Good for you." Mommy nodded approvingly, but her mouth twitched. "Poor Esther Leah; I imagine she was disappointed."

Bracha Ora shrugged. "I won fair and square."

"Of course you did, but to come so close and then not win can be hard," Mommy said. She paused thoughtfully and met Bracha Ora's eyes.

"I worked hard," Bracha Ora insisted.

"I know you did," Mommy said softly. "I'm sure Esther Leah did, too." After a moment of silence, Mommy continued on a cheerful note, "What comes next? Do you get a prize?"

"Not for this spelling bee, but next week there's going to be a grand spelling bee for all the third grade finalists in the school. If I win *that*, I get a big prize—a free book from Bellers' Bookstore!"

Bracha Ora twirled in a circle, her eyes gleaming. She could picture herself winning the grand spelling bee...stepping up to a podium in front of a large crowd...lowering her eyes as she was handed a fabulous award... Her heart sang at the thought.

Mommy's eyebrows lifted at that. "Wow, that's really something."

"I have to win! It would be so exciting! See you later, Ma. I'm going to study more spelling words!"

"Good luck," Mommy wished her. As she stirred the vegetable soup her smile faded, and a concerned frown tugged at her lips.

For the next week, Bracha Ora's nose seemed stuck inside her spelling book. Even while eating or walking, she was still reviewing and memorizing as many words as she could.

Finally, when she felt her brain could not handle even one more second of studying, the big day arrived. The finalists from each of the five third grade classes were invited to go on stage. Silence filled the auditorium as students and teachers wondered who would be the big winner.

"Please spell identity," Mrs. Milah began.

Like a ping-pong ball flying over a net, questions and answers shot forth, pinging across the stage with perfect aim.

"How about the word quarter?"

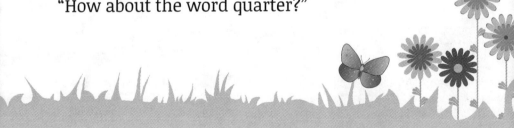

"Please spell penguin."

Leah crinkled her forehead. "P-e-n-g-i-n," she ventured.

"No, Leah, I'm sorry. Bracha Ora, do you know?"

Bracha Ora quickly nodded, ticking off the letters on her fingers as she spoke.

"Excellent! Miriam, can you spell the word ostrich?"

Miriam's face turned white as snow, and she blinked rapidly, a sure sign that she was very nervous.

"Miriam, do you know?" Mrs. Milah repeated in a soft but firm voice.

Shaking her head, Miriam rose from her seat and descended from the stage, blinking rapidly and keeping her eyes pinned to the floor.

After several more rounds of increasingly difficult words, only two girls remained on stage: Bracha Ora and Shifra. You could almost hear the collective intake of breath as everyone waited to

see who would be the winner. Bracha Ora wiped clammy palms on her skirt and whispered a quick *tefillah*. She wanted so badly to win, and she had worked so hard.

"Shifra?" Mrs. Milah looked her in the eye. "Spell refrigerator."

"R-e-f-r-i," Shifra began, and Mrs. Milah nodded encouragingly.

Then silence.

This was the moment Bracha Ora had been waiting for. She knew how to spell refrigerator! *Oh, please, Hashem, let Shifra not know and give me the chance! Imagine me, being the winner of the grand spelling bee! I'll get any book I want at Bellers' Bookstore!* Bracha Ora tapped her toes, stared at her fingernails, and waited. As the moments ticked by, Shifra began to squirm. Suddenly, Bracha Ora took a look at Shifra's face.

Shifra's brown eyes swam with sadness. Bracha Ora knew why. Shifra's mother had never been well, and to top that off, her father had just lost his job. Shifra often came to school late and untidy, her shirt untucked and stained. Her wavy hair flew in all different directions, looking like it had never had been brushed. Most girls stayed away from Shifra because of her unpleasant appearance. She didn't do well in most subjects in school, either. Usually, when a teacher called on her, she didn't know the right answer.

I know how to spell refrigerator, Bracha Ora thought. *I know it!*

"All right, then," Mrs. Milah was saying. "Bracha Ora, do *you* know how to spell refrigerator?"

Bracha Ora glanced again at Shifra, then at Mrs. Milah, and Bracha Ora made her decision. She looked down and swallowed hard. "No, Mrs. Milah."

"Really?" Mrs. Milah looked somewhat surprised. *A moment ago Bracha Ora had looked like she was bursting to answer the question*, she mused. "We'll have to try a different question."

Rifling through her cards, Mrs. Milah chose one. "How about the word dictionary?"

Bracha Ora wanted to jump out of her seat. She knew that answer, too—she was sure of it!

"Do either of you know?"

Bracha Ora took a deep breath, but she slowly shook her head back and forth.

"Shifra?"

Shifra's eyebrows were furrowed, and she wore a look of intense concentration.

"Is it d-i-c-t-i-o-n-a-r-y?" she asked tentatively.

"Correct!" Mrs. Milah exclaimed. "Mazel tov, Shifra! You just won the grand spelling bee! Brilliant job! And Bracha Ora, you, too, should feel very proud. You held out so well. Let's have a hand for our winner and our runner-up, please!"

Bracha Ora ran over to Shifra with a wide smile. "Mazel tov!" she wished her warmly.

"Thanks," Shifra said, and her eyes glowed like a thousand light bulbs.

When Bracha Ora walked home after school that day, the world seemed splashed with bright colors. Roses and tulips smiled up at her, and cardinals and bluebirds chirped a friendly greeting. Her heart was light; she felt even better than on the day she had won the class bee.

Why am I in such a good mood? Bracha Ora wondered. The answer came in a flash as she recalled Shifra's happiness. *I may have lost the grand spelling bee*, she realized, *but instead I won something much more important.*

"Eye" Care for You

"Tzippy Levov, please come in," Dr. Ayin's receptionist called, her eyes roving the waiting area.

Mommy and Tzippy got up and followed her lead to an examination room.

"How's everything?" Dr. Ayin greeted them cheerily. "Are your glasses working well for you?"

"Well," Tzippy said, "sometimes I don't see so well even with them on."

"Hmm." Dr. Ayin furrowed his bushy eyebrows and read through some paperwork. "Well, let's take a look and see what's going on."

He began showing Tzippy letter charts and asked her to read them out loud.

"Does number one seem clearer, or do you like two better?"

Tzippy leaned forward and squinted through the big black machine, trying her hardest to read the chart up on the wall.

"Two, I think," she said.

"Okay, read the bottom line."

"A-D-L-P-Q-W," Tzippy said, but the letters were really B-O-I-R-D-U. Dr. Ayin pursed his lips. He continued the examination for another few minutes before flicking off the light switch and moving the machine away from Tzippy.

"Tzippy, your right eye sees perfectly with this prescription," Dr. Ayin explained, pulling his swivel chair closer to her, "but your left eye is having some trouble. I see this all the time—it's called lazy eye. Your left eye is weak and doesn't see so well, so it goes on vacation and lets the right eye do all the work."

"Just like me," Tzippy said with a grin. "I also like vacations."

Dr. Ayin chuckled. "Well, here's what we're going to do. We're going to try to make your left eye stronger, so that you'll have two helpful eyes. I'll give you a patch to wear during the day, and you put it over your right eye. Here's how to use it." He showed Tzippy how to slide the patch under the right lens of her glasses. "This way, your left eye has to work—it won't have a choice. Since your right eye will be covered, you won't be able to see through that eye while you're wearing the patch.

"Now is there a certain type of animal or picture that you would like on your patch? I have a whole bunch of fun characters to choose from."

Ambling over to a shelf on the wall, Dr. Ayin pulled down a basket of patches. There was a huge assortment. Tzippy noticed yellow ones with cats and dogs, pink ones with princesses, blue ones with trucks, and other colored ones with a variety of animals on them.

"Which one do you like?"

Tzippy chose a purple patch with a picture of a raccoon.

"He's just like me," she pointed out. "You see, he is also wearing a patch on his eyes."

Mommy and Dr. Ayin both laughed out loud. The raccoon, with a black rim around its eyes, did look like it might have just seen a raccoon optometrist.

Tzippy and Mommy came home, and Tzippy darted to the mirror to look at her reflection. Her bright smile still seemed the same. Her nose and freckles hadn't changed a bit, but when she lifted her eyes to stare at the top portion of her face, she caught her breath. Only one sparkly hazel eye peered back at her, while the other one was covered by a raccoon patch!

I don't look normal, Tzippy worried. *What will my friends think?*

While her thoughts spun with different ways that her friends might greet the "new Tzippy," she slowly trudged upstairs to her room. Suddenly she marched—BAM!—headlong into a wall, tripping and falling to the floor from the impact.

"Hey," she demanded angrily, "who put that wall there, anyway?"

Rubbing her aching head, Tzippy whimpered. A few seconds later she got up, headed down the hall to her room, and opened the door.

"Hey, why are you barging into my room without knocking?" Her older sister, Chaya, glared at her with accusing eyes.

"Oh," Tzippy said, backing out. "Sorry."

She shook her head in confusion. How had she mixed up her room with her sister's? That had never happened before.

Tzippy finally got to her room, and with a loud sigh, she reached for a library book and climbed onto her bed. Another unwelcome surprise was

waiting for her. When she opened the book to the first page, the letters swam dizzyingly in front of her, and she couldn't read a single word.

Why are the words so foggy? she wondered, squinting desperately to help them come into focus. It didn't work. Bringing the book almost up to her nose also didn't help. *What's going on?*

With her heart sinking to her stomach, Tzippy remembered Dr. Ayin's explanation, and she understood what was happening. Covering her strong eye would force her weak eye to work and help her see, but it would take time until the muscles in her left eye became stronger. Right now those muscles were so weak, they were causing her to have all sorts of vision problems. Frustrated, Tzippy threw down her book.

Immediately her thoughts turned to school the next day. When her friends would see her eye patch for the first time, they might make fun of her. Suddenly, fat tears began trickling down her cheeks.

It's bad enough that I'm having a hard time seeing with this patch, but to appear in public this way, looking like a raccoon? Tzippy felt as if dozens of large butterflies were flapping their wings back and forth inside her stomach.

"Mommy, I can't go to school like this," Tzippy said after dinner. "All the girls will laugh at me." Angrily, she pulled the patch off of her eye and threw it across the room.

"I understand, this is really hard for you," Mommy said. "Tzippy, don't you want two healthy, strong eyes to help you see for the rest of your life, *b'ezras Hashem*?"

Tzippy nodded, blinking back tears. "Yes, but why does it have to be so hard?" she asked, sniffling.

Mommy put an arm around her shoulder. "Oh, Tzippy," Mommy said. "If I could make it any easier for you, you know I would, but the sooner you start wearing that patch, the better your eye will see. Who

knows? Maybe it will work fast and you won't have to wear it for very long, but that will only happen if you agree to wear it."

After Tzippy was tucked into bed, Mommy put in a call to Tzippy's teacher.

"Mrs. Mabit, this is Mrs. Levov calling—Tzippy's mother."

"Oh, hi, Mrs. Levov, how are you?"

"*Baruch Hashem*, thank you," Mommy replied, and then began telling Mrs. Mabit about Tzippy's eye condition and how she would have to wear a patch during the day.

"I see," Mrs. Mabit said thoughtfully. "So she's embarrassed to face the other girls with her patch."

"Yes. She's coming to school with it for the first time tomorrow, and I wanted you to know what's going on."

"I have an idea," Mrs. Mabit said, her eyes lighting up. She hoped her plan would work, but she would need Mrs. Levov's cooperation.

"I think we can help Tzippy with this, but can you bring her about ten minutes late tomorrow?"

"Sure," Mrs. Levov agreed, surprised by the request. Normally teachers don't like students to come late, but if that's what the teacher wanted, then that's what she would do.

Bright and early the next morning Tzippy moaned. "Ooooh. My big toe is hurting so badly. I can't walk!"

"I'm sorry." Mommy's voice was soft but firm. "I guess you'll have to hop around or limp today. You can't miss school because of your eye patch, even though I know you would love to."

Within the hour, Mommy was pulling their red minivan into the parking lot of Tzippy's school. Tzippy's face looked like a thundercloud waiting to burst.

"Have a wonderful day, Tzippy," Mommy said.

Tzippy sniffed, and a large tear rolled down her cheek. "Mommy, what if the girls make fun of me?"

Mommy's warm chocolate eyes locked with Tzippy's. "It will be okay. Your friends will like you just as much even though you're wearing a patch."

A sob caught in Tzippy's throat. "But they'll think I'm weird!" she cried.

Mommy wrapped Tzippy in a big hug. "No, they won't. They'll think you're very smart for taking care of your eye and helping it get stronger. You'll see."

Tzippy sadly waved goodbye to her mother and, like a large, awkward turtle, plodded up the stairs and into the school building. Her head was lowered so no one could see how ridiculous she looked wearing a patch over her eye.

"Hi, Tzippy!" her class greeted her when she walked into the room.

Surprised by the eager greeting, Tzippy forgot to keep her eyes peeled to the ground. When she looked up, she couldn't believe what she was seeing. Nineteen sets of eyes gazed

back at her. And every single one of them had one eye covered with a patch.

Tzippy's mouth fell open, and she exploded into a fit of giggles. "You...you are the best classmates ever!" she managed to say when she was finally able to speak.

"We didn't want you to feel different," Rivky said, smiling widely.

"Come sit," Elana invited, motioning Tzippy toward her regular seat. "It's not so easy to look around with just one eye. How do you do it?"

Tzippy beamed and quickly took her seat. "You know, it's not so bad," she said. "I think I'm starting to get used to it already."

"I like your raccoon," Shevi said.

"I like your princess," Tzippy replied with a grin.

"Okay, girls," Mrs. Mabit began, "it's nice to see everyone. Let's get started."

They all sat down in their seats and

took out their siddurim. Nineteen students quietly removed their eye patches. The twentieth student kept it on and lifted her chin high. Because she knew these girls cared about her and were her friends, so what difference did a little patch make?

Wait Up, Chippy!

Adina was sitting in Dr. Leibowitz's waiting room, waiting her turn. She was going to camp for the summer and needed a check-up so that all the medical forms could be filled out.

She stared at the clock, its hands barely seemed to move. Then she glanced at the aquarium, watching as the colorful fish glided through the water. Looking up at the clock, she noted that two minutes had passed.

"Ma, when are they going to call me already?"

"As soon as it's our turn, honey," her mother replied.

"But this is ridiculous! We've been waiting here forever! I have stuff to do. I'm going to tell the receptionist."

"Adina," Mommy warned, "that wouldn't be polite. I know it's hard to wait, but we don't have a choice."

"Maybe we should leave and come back another day!" Adina pouted, crossing her arms over her chest.

"And then have to wait all over again. What would that help? I have an idea. I wrote a story for a children's magazine. How about listening to it and giving me your opinion?"

"Okay, I guess," Adina agreed. It wasn't like she had anything else to do.

"Great!" Mommy said with a smile. Her blue eyes sparkled as she began the story...

●●●

Scampering up the side of a tall oak tree, Chippy Chipmunk peered inside his cozy home and greeted his Ima with a cheerful hello.

"Mm, something smells delicious." His nose twitched with delight as he pictured his favorite acorn pie, steaming hot and fresh from the oven. "When will it be ready?"

"In about an hour or so," Ima answered, looking over her shoulder at her eager little boy. "Why don't you go do something while you wait, and I'll call you when it's ready?"

Chippy stamped his foot, and a large scowl turned his lips downward. "Why does it have to take so long? I hate waiting!"

Stomping off to a corner of their snug den, Chippy curled himself into a little ball and sulked.

"I have some extra acorns if you're hungry," Ima offered, laying a soft paw on Chippy's shoulder.

"I don't want acorns!" Chippy insisted. "I want pie, NOW!"

Shaking her head, Ima went back to the kitchen to work on supper.

Just then the phone rang. Chippy went to answer it.

"Hi, Chippy? It's Bubby. How are you?"

"*Baruch Hashem*, Bubby." Chippy's voice was quiet, and Bubby understood that he was not feeling very chipper today.

"Chippy, I sent you a surprise in the mail. Very soon, Tall Tail Delivery will bring it straight to your tree trunk. Let me know when you get it, okay, Chip?"

"Thanks, Bubby! I will," Chippy answered, a bright smile chasing away his frown. *I wonder what Bubby sent me. Could it be the new camera I've been wanting? Or a watch with light-up numbers? Or a CD player?* All the things on his wish list marched across the path of his imagination, and his heart thumped with excitement.

For the next few days, Chippy watched and waited for his present to come. He sat with his nose pressed

against the window, his every muscle poised to run downstairs and greet the delivery truck as soon as it arrived. Trucks kept driving up and down his street, but not one stopped to bring him a package. Poor Chippy. His shoulders slumped, and his tail drooped. Why was the wait so hard and so long?

"Hi, Chippy, how was your day?" Ima greeted him the next day when he came home from school.

"Did my package come?" he asked eagerly, his brown eyes shining with excitement.

"I'm afraid not," Ima replied, and Chippy heaved a big sigh.

"Today you have a dentist appointment," Ima told Chippy, handing him some seeds and fruit for a snack. Chippy ate quickly, and then it was time to go. Putting his small paw in Ima's large one, the two headed to Dr. Shain's office.

As they walked, they passed a large goose sitting on a nest.

"Hi, Mrs. Goose," Chippy said. "What are you doing?"

"I'm keeping my babies warm," she replied, fluttering her wings and sitting up proudly. "I have to sit here for about six weeks until all six eggs are ready to hatch."

Chippy whistled. "Six weeks!" he repeated. "What a long time! Don't you wish they could come out right away, so you wouldn't have to just sit and wait?"

"Oh," she honked, "this is my job! I'm proud to take care of my babies. I don't mind at all. It gives me time to think about what I want to teach them once they're born, and how excited I will be to see them."

"Well, have fun," Chippy said before they continued on their way. "I'm sure glad I'm not a goose," he added, and his mother and Mrs. Goose chuckled.

When they arrived at Dr. Shain's office, the waiting room was filled to the brim with noisy chipmunks and squirrels of all sizes.

"Wow, it's crowded," Ima observed, finding two seats at the far end of the waiting room.

"Would you like to read until it's our turn?" She offered Chippy a choice of books from the *Burrow* series, a special collection of chapter stories for young chipmunks and squirrels.

"No!" Chippy's eyebrows scrunched together, and his angry scowl was back. "Why do we have to wait? Dr. Shain has to call us in right now, or I'm leaving!"

"You're staying right here, young man," Ima replied sternly, placing a firm paw on Chippy's shoulder. "Waiting can be hard, but it's part of life. Still, you can make the wait pleasant if you try."

"I don't understand why the dentist can't just call us in right away," Chippy whined. "It's our appointment time, isn't it?"

"Yes, it is, but sometimes other patients take longer than the dentist thought they would, and then he runs late," Ima explained.

"It's not fair!" Chippy cried.

"Dr. Shain is just trying to do his best to take care of everyone," Ima said. "Now why don't you choose a book to read?"

Chippy chose a book and tried to read, but it was hard to concentrate. His mind was buzzing with angry thoughts about waiting, and the uselessness of it all.

If I had my way, Chippy thought, *I would invent a world where no one had to wait for anything. What an amazing world that would be…*

Chippy looked around and found himself in a beautiful garden. Carpets of bright green grass spread out in front of him. Tall oak, fern, and dogwood trees waved their branches in a gentle breeze, and flowers in every hue of the rainbow smiled at him from every direction.

"Welcome to Rodents' Paradise," Chippy read on a colorful sign posted at the garden entrance.

Hmm, I wonder what this is, Chippy mused, walking up to a large machine that had different colored buttons with pictures of his favorite types of food.

"Seed stew," Chippy read out loud. "Well, why not?" He pushed the button. There was a whirring sound, and before he could count to three, out popped a large bowl brimming with a flavorful stew.

Chippy smacked his lips and sat down on a bench to enjoy his lunch. "Mm, delicious!" he said happily.

"Now for a drink. The apricot smoothie looks good." With another flick of a button, the smoothie was ready, and Chippy gulped it down happily.

"Now for dessert." Chippy peered at each of the pictures before making his choice.

"Pecan pie coming right up," the machine said, and in an instant a ready-made pie popped out, right into Chippy's waiting paws.

After eating his fill, Chippy wanted to explore the rest of the garden. Walking past some pink rose bushes, Chippy came to a beautiful tent. "Step inside and welcome Shabbos," he read.

Curious, Chippy opened the tent, and what he saw took his breath away. A beautiful table was set for Shabbos, the candles were lit, and all the food was laid out. It was so wonderful that he was ready to jump right into Shabbos, but something was bothering him. Furrowing his brow, he stood still and tried to figure out what it was. *Ah, that's it! I'm not ready for Shabbos yet. I haven't bathed, I don't have my Shabbos tie, and I haven't had a chance to study the* parshah. *Shabbos can't just come in without warning, I need time!*

"Not ready for Shabbos yet?" A large squirrel, with big, black-rimmed glasses and the bushiest tail Chippy had ever seen, read his thoughts. "No problem, no problem at all. You're in Rodents' Paradise, remember?" And he stretched out his paw and pointed to the next booth.

"Push button for an instant shower and come out wearing Shabbos clothes," Chippy read. *Hm, I should've known.* He pushed the button, and in a shake of a squirrel's tail, he was squeaky clean and dressed for Shabbos.

Well, now I look Shabbosdik, Chippy mused, as he stepped out of the booth, *but something still doesn't feel quite right.*

He stepped back into the Shabbos tent and enjoyed a wonderful Shabbos there. The food was tasty, the *divrei Torah* and *zemiros* were beautiful, and Chippy enjoyed a snuggly Shabbos nap. When he woke up, something was still bothering him, almost like a buzzing fly that wouldn't leave him alone, yet he couldn't figure out what it was. *Shalosh seudos*, Havdalah, and a relaxing night's sleep on a soft mossy cushion under a tall tree ended the peaceful day.

The next morning, as the sun painted the sky in purples and pinks, a voice called out to him. "Step right up, Mr. Chipmunk, step over here! Get your elementary school diploma, no school necessary. That's right! We pronounce you an elementary school graduate without the wait!"

"But-but, how can I graduate if I haven't learned everything I need to know?" Chippy sputtered.

The squirrel who was talking to him shook his head. "Oh, did I forget to tell you? Just push that button over there"—he pointed to a button with a picture of a diploma on it—"and you will have all the information you need, without the bother of spending a whole bunch of years waiting to graduate."

Chippy stepped forward, pushed the button, and suddenly his head was filled, all the way to the tips of his pointed ears, with oodles of information. He knew his Chumash, he knew his Gemara, and he knew how to write an essay. Wow! How neat was that! Chippy walked away, feeling a little taller and a lot smarter, but something was bothering him.

Right around the corner, next to a fir tree that seemed to touch the sky, a large goose was minding her goslings.

"Mazel tov, Mrs. Goose," Chippy called out. "How long did you have to sit on your nest before your eggs hatched?"

"Oh, there was no wait at all," Mrs. Goose honked. "The eggs hatched right after I laid them." She paused for a moment, and then added, "A little wait might have been nice. I could have read the book on *Tips for Raising Well-Mannered Goslings*, but I didn't have time." Her eyes looked a little sad, Chippy noticed, as if she felt that waiting would have helped her become a better mother goose. With a shake of his furry head, Chippy moved on.

"Wow! What's this?" His eyes opened wide as he stared at the most interesting building he had ever seen. The building was the shape and color of a giant chipmunk holding a paintbrush and easel. On the easel were the words: Design Your Own Artwork.

Curious, Chippy went inside. There were hundreds of buttons to push: buttons for colors, buttons for glitter, buttons for sequins and beads, and more.

"Well, why not?" Chippy said. He decided to create a picture of a little chipmunk in a garden staring up at a rainbow.

He pushed some buttons, and then—poof! In the time it takes to say 'chipmunk,' his picture popped out of a slot.

"It's beautiful," Chippy marveled, brushing his paw along the artwork and admiring the bright colors. "It even kind of looks like me! Maybe I'll give it to Ima."

Holding the paper tightly in his paws, Chippy took two flying jumps forward, but something was still bothering him. He stopped midjump for a minute to think. He looked at the picture once more. Nothing wrong there, so what was that funny feeling he had inside?

After a moment, Chippy gave up trying to figure out what was bothering him. *Maybe it will come to me later,* he thought. *I want to finish exploring before it's time to go home.*

"Mitzvah booth," he read, hopping into an elevator. Whoosh! The doors closed, and he was whisked up to a tree house built in the branches of a mighty tree.

A very old chipmunk greeted him with a nod. "Very good, very good," he said, "I am pleased that you want to do mitzvos. Go ahead, sonny,

pick your mitzvah and see how fast it will get done."

Chippy walked over to the mitzvah machine and stared. So many choices! There was a picture of a siddur, a Chumash, helping his mother in the kitchen or his father with yard work, carrying a package for a very old man. Why, he could be here all day if he wanted to do everything!

The old chipmunk peered at him through his bifocals. "What's taking you so long, sonny? Push a button! You know there's no waiting around in Rodents' Paradise!"

Chippy pushed the siddur button. In a burst of light and a quick ring, he had somehow *davened* the entire Shacharis. A paper appeared with his name and a large smiley face next to a siddur picture.

"I'm finished already? But I didn't even have a chance to think about what I was saying!" Chippy felt a little sad, and his tail drooped. "I'll try another mitzvah."

He pushed the yard work button and saw a quick slide show of him raking leaves next to Abba. In a flash, the leaves were raked and

bagged, and Abba was smiling proudly at him. Now he had another smiley next to his name, showing the mitzvah he had just done.

This is really neat! Chippy grinned, but that feeling was back. What was it that was bothering him? He sat down on the ground, cupped his chin in his paws, and had a good think. Suddenly everything became clear. It felt like he had been sitting in a dark room, and suddenly the room was filled with golden light.

As hard as waiting can be, it's really a good thing, Chippy thought. *It gives a chipmunk time to prepare and get ready for things that are really important. There's something else, too, when you do something with your own two paws, you have a good feeling inside. It's the feeling that comes from working hard at something and then seeing the results. That feeling is just not there when it's done for you, chick-chock.*

"Okay," Chippy murmured. "I'm ready to go home now."

"Really?" chorused all the chipmunks and squirrels that had gathered around him. "But life is so easy here.

Are you sure you don't want to stay here forever?"

"I'm sure," Chippy answered firmly. And he headed straight for the tall white gates.

Someone was calling his name. Chippy woke up from his sleep. "Chippy Chipmunk, please come back!" It was Dr. Shain's nurse.

"I'm sorry for the long wait," the nurse apologized to Chippy and his mother as she led them into an examination room. "Dr. Shain had an emergency."

"Oh, that's okay," Chippy said calmly. "I just had a little nap in the waiting room, and I had the most amazing dream. You know, you can do so many useful things while you wait."

Ima lifted her eyebrows in surprise, and her mouth formed a round circle as she looked at Chippy. Who was this patient chipmunk at her side? Where had her impatient Chippy gone?

When Ima and Chippy got home, Chippy found a surprise waiting at the foot of their tree: a wrapped box that had his name on it!

Eagerly opening the box, Chippy found a beautiful book called *A Chipmunk's Guide to Waiting*. The book contained a bunch of stories about chipmunks that had to wait for something, and it gave many ideas for how that "waiting time" could be productively spent.

"Ima, when is supper going to be ready?" Chippy asked, feeling his stomach rumble. Ima was puttering around in the kitchen, making loud clanking noises with pots and pans.

"Oh, in about an hour," she answered. "Do you have a way to keep yourself busy?"

Do I have a way to keep busy! Chippy almost laughed out loud at the question. *I have so many things I can do! I can help Ima, I can read my new book...* And then another idea popped into his head.

"Ima, I'll be right back and I'll set the table, but first I have to make a phone call."

Taking the phone in his paw, Chippy dialed Bubby's number.

"Hello?" Bubby's voice sounded warm and loving and close, almost like she was right in the tree house with him.

"Hi, Bubby, it's Chippy. I wanted to thank you for my present and tell you I love you, and for that, I couldn't wait!"

•••

"Wow, Mommy, great story!"

"Thanks, Adina. I thought you might like it."

"Adina Hertz," a nurse called, opening the door and nodding in her direction.

"I apologize for the wait," the nurse said as she directed them to an examining room. "Dr. Leibowitz was really backed up today."

"It's no problem," Adina said, giving her mother a secret wink. "Waiting is part of life."

Saved by Sandwiches

"Hi, Ma!" Baruch and Nachi bounded inside one Sunday afternoon, hot, tired, and hungry after yeshivah. "What's for lunch?"

"Grilled cheese and salad," Mommy answered with a smile. "It's all ready."

Baruch and Nachi looked at each other, their smiles fading.

"Um, I'm not so hungry for grilled cheese," Baruch said. "I think I'll have cereal instead."

"Me, too," Nachi agreed, following Baruch to the pantry and pulling out a box of Chex.

"Why?" Mommy frowned at the boys. "You like grilled cheese. Why won't you eat it?"

"Because then we'll have to *bentch*," Baruch explained, pouring cereal into his bowl.

"Yeah," Nachi said. "It takes such a long time. We've got stuff to do."

Shaking her head in disappointment, Mommy wrapped up the sandwiches. She hoped her husband would eat them later, so they wouldn't go to waste. Letting out a sigh, Mommy sat down at the table and began eating her own lunch.

"Guess what?" Mommy said. Baruch and Nachi looked up. "Remember we talked about going boating?" They nodded. "Well, I found a place to go canoeing that's not too far away. When you're finished eating, prepare some snacks, and we'll go there, okay?"

"Yippee! We're going canoeing! Thank you, Mommy!"

Polishing off their cereal in a jiffy, Baruch and Nachi zoomed to the pantry to prepare some snacks for the trip. Popcorn, granola

bars, and large green apples made their way into a tote bag, and before you could say "Let's go boating," the boys were strapped in their seatbelts ready for action.

"Are we there yet?" Nachi asked five minutes into the drive.

"We are exactly five minutes closer than we were five minutes ago," Tatty remarked.

"Let's play the ABC game," Baruch suggested.

Looking at license plates and signs that they passed, they took turns finding the letters of the alphabet in chronological order.

"Are we there yet?" Nachi inquired the second the game ended.

"No, but we're fifteen minutes closer," Mommy answered.

Both boys groaned and shifted in their seats.

"Time for another game," Nachi said. "How about geography?"

Finally Baruch and Nachi let out a cheer as they

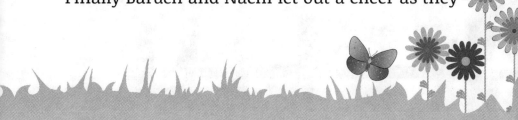

pulled into the parking lot of Bernie's Boat Rentals. After all the papers had been signed, and they had trekked down to the lake to choose their boats, Baruch remembered something.

"Tatty, I left my Crocs in the car," he said. "Can I have your key so I can get them?"

"Okay," Tatty said, handing the car key to Baruch. "But please—"

"I know, I know, I'll be careful," Baruch finished his sentence.

Everyone laughed as Baruch dashed toward the car. Quickly changing out of his sneakers, he slipped into his Crocs and locked the car door again. He plunged the key deep into his pocket and raced back to join the family.

Clambering into two canoes, lifejackets buckled snugly, Tatty and Baruch, and Mommy and Nachi paddled down the river.

"Race you!" Tatty and Baruch called out.

"You're on!" Mommy and Nachi replied,

dipping their oars quickly in and out of the water.

Mommy and Nachi sped ahead. After about fifteen minutes, Tatty and Baruch declared them the winners.

The tired sailors decided it was time to relax, and they allowed the current to carry them forward. A bright sun beamed down, and the swish of the water was soothing, until Tatty and Baruch's canoe smashed into something.

"Oof!" Tatty said. "What happened?"

"A rock," Baruch answered, sticking his hand into the cold river and feeling a hard, slimy rock. "We're stuck."

Tatty tried to row forward, but the entire back of their boat was lodged on the rock and refused to budge. There was also another boulder wedging them in on the side. Baruch pushed hard against the rock, and the canoe slid backward; but then it waffled back to where it had been. There was no doubt about it. They were stuck.

"Trouble?" Mommy called from across the river as she edged closer.

"Be careful," Tatty warned. "We don't want you getting stuck, too."

Suddenly, Baruch had an idea. He spied a long branch a few feet away, and decided to grab it. He figured he could use it to help them out of this mess. He stood up and reached forward, determined to set them free. In a flash, the canoe rolled over, spilling Tatty and Baruch into the lake with a loud splash.

Two ducks quacked as they glided by, no doubt wondering about these strange-looking "ducks."

Sputtering and laughing, Tatty helped Baruch climb back inside the boat. Then Tatty shoved the canoe off the rock before rejoining Baruch.

"I wish I had my camera," Nachi said, giggling.

"That's one way to take a bath," Mommy added.

The rest of the ride was calm, and after

another half hour of peaceful sailing, they arrived back at the dock.

"I'm starving!" Baruch said, rubbing his stomach. "Good thing we have snacks in the car."

"Yeah!" Nachi seconded.

"Baruch, do you have my car key?" Tatty asked. "You didn't give it back to me."

"I sure do," Baruch said, fishing in his pocket. His face turned pale when his fingers met up with nothing but each other. No key!

"Um," Baruch sputtered, "I hate to give you bad news, but..." Without saying another word, he lifted his pocket and turned it inside out. Three pairs of eyes stared in dismay at the empty lining.

"It must have fallen into the lake when we fell in," Baruch said mournfully. "What do we do now?"

Tatty scrolled through the contacts on his cell phone. "I have the number of a locksmith here. I'll try calling him."

"It'll be about an hour before I can get to you," the locksmith informed Tatty.

"But I'm starving!" Nachi complained.

"What are you complaining about?" Baruch growled. "At least you're not soaking wet."

"Boys!" Mommy said, giving them a stern look.

"This is all your fault," Nachi whispered to Baruch.

Baruch's face turned red, but before he could respond, a car pulled into the parking lot, and the Feldmans, close family friends, piled out.

"Hi there!" The Feldmans greeted them cheerfully. "Funny meeting you here. Did you have fun?"

"We had a great time," Mommy and Tatty replied.

"Until we got locked out of our car," Nachi added, glaring at Baruch.

"Oh, no!" Mrs. Feldman cried.

"The locksmith is on the way," Tatty told her, "so *b'ezras Hashem* we should be fine."

"Are you hungry?" Mrs. Feldman asked. "We have plenty of sandwiches with us."

"Awesome!" Baruch and Nachi shouted.

A few minutes later, Mommy, Tatty, Baruch, and Nachi were sitting at a picnic table, enjoying fresh peanut butter and jelly sandwiches.

"I just realized," Mommy said, looking carefully at Baruch and Nachi, "you must feel bad that you're eating bread. Now you're going to have to *bentch*, and it will take a little while."

"Are you kidding?" Baruch said, grinning as he reached for another sandwich. "It's so amazing how Hashem sent us food right when we needed it."

"Yeah," Nachi said, licking his lips. "What were the chances that the Feldmans would show up here, of all places, right now—*and* have extra food on them? Taking a few minutes to thank Hashem after what He did for us...what's the big deal?"

The next day, when Baruch and Nachi came home from yeshivah, a delicious smell wafted toward them from the kitchen.

"Hi, Ma," Baruch called, swinging the door open. "What's for dinner?"

"Something smells really good," Nachi commented.

"French toast and vegetable soup," Mommy said. "How does that sound?"

"Terrific!" they said, dashing over to the sink to wash.

"I hope you don't mind the bread," Mommy said. "I had a lot of leftover challah, and that makes really good French toast."

"I've been thinking about *bentching*," Nachi said, contentedly chomping French toast smothered in maple syrup. "Since our trip yesterday, I realize we owe Hashem so much. I mean, He does everything for us all the time."

"Yeah," Baruch chimed in. "So spending a few minutes to say thank you for a good meal—it's worth it!"

"I'm proud of you, boys!" Mommy exclaimed.

After they *bentched* and cleared their plates,

Baruch glanced at the clock. Turning to Nachi, he asked, "Wanna ride bikes?"

"Sure," Nachi answered. "We still have time before it gets dark."

"Have fun," Mommy called after them.

Just when they got to the door, Baruch stopped short. "Ma?" he called out.

"Yes, Baruch?"

"Thanks for dinner. It was the best."

"Yeah," Nachi agreed. "It was really yummy. Thank you!"

Smiling, Mommy reached for a *bentcher* and sat down. She wanted to thank Hashem for the delicious meal she too had just eaten—and for her two wonderful boys who were maturing more and more each day.

The Dancer

Shifra Goldman loved to dance. Any time she saw a leaf sailing through the air, she wished she could join hands with it and pirouette gracefully, as if she, too, were flying. The only problem was, Shifra had two left feet.

When Mrs. Boxman, her fourth grade teacher, announced that the two fourth grade classes would be putting on a Pesach performance together, Shifra's heart leaped. Mrs. Boxman stated there would be a play, a choir, and a dance group. How she wished she could be part of the dance group!

"Of course we have a props committee, too, which is very important," Mrs. Boxman added. "You may choose what you most enjoy doing, and we'll start practicing tomorrow, *im yirtzeh Hashem*."

"What do you want to do?" Batya asked Shifra at lunch.

"I want to dance," Shifra replied quickly. "I love dancing."

"I think I want to be in the play," Batya said thoughtfully, munching her peanut butter and jelly sandwich.

Pushing her chair back, Shifra got up to refill her water bottle when she bumped into someone passing right behind her.

"Oof!" both girls exclaimed as the two of them landed on the floor in a tangle of arms, legs, and some leftover lunch.

"Look what you did!" Chani yelled at Shifra, pointing to a big ketchup stain on her light blue shirt. "You're such a klutz! Why can't you look where you're going?"

Shifra's face turned as red as the stain,

which she stared at in dismay. "S-sorry," she mumbled.

"A lot of good that does," Chani muttered, shooting one last glare at Shifra before marching her way toward the sink.

I said I was sorry, Shifra thought, watching her go. *Why does she have to get so upset?*

Shifra tossed and turned that night, her mind busily spinning dreams of herself dancing across the stage. She could hardly wait for the first practice, which was scheduled to begin right after school the next day.

The next morning, Shifra yawned her way through her classes, as the hours slowly ticked by. Yet by the time the bell sounded, Shifra's tiredness had vanished, and her heart was pumping a mile a minute.

Finally all the fourth grade girls headed toward the auditorium. Two other teachers were already there, one to teach the choir, and the other to direct

the play. Mrs. Boxman herself was going to direct the dance group. Patiently she showed the dance girls the first set of steps, and Shifra eagerly tried to mimic the moves.

"Ouch!" Dena roared. "Shifra, that was my toe! Can't you watch what you're doing?"

"Oh! Oops!" Shifra jumped, startled by Dena's reaction.

"Hey, watch it!" Leah yelped as Shifra rammed into her side.

Mrs. Boxman stared at the scene in dismay, her face cupped in her hands, her eyes wide.

"Let's begin with a different dance," she suggested, positioning the girls in several lines. Maybe if they were a little further apart, things would go easier. That's what she hoped, but her hopes crashed when Shifra flung her arms out a little too wide, smacking both girls on either side of her.

"That's it!" Chedva huffed, arms folded across her chest. "If Shifra's in dance, then I'm out."

"Me, too," Tzirel seconded, rubbing the red splotch on her cheek.

"Girls, please calm down," Mrs. Boxman said. "The first practice is always hard. Everyone will get the hang of it sooner or later—you'll see. Now please wait near the front doors for your parents to come pick you up."

"Klutz!" Chedva whispered as she passed Shifra.

"You do not know how to dance!" Tzirel added.

Tears welled up in Shifra's eyes. *Maybe she couldn't dance? Maybe the girls were right?*

"Is everything okay, Shifra?" Mommy asked, when she noticed that Shifra was unusually quiet.

Shifra nodded, not trusting herself to speak. She didn't really want to talk about what had happened, but she was thinking about switching groups. The problem was, a part in the play frightened her, and she didn't really enjoy singing. Maybe she should just join the props group?

A wail sounded from upstairs, and Shifra ran to get her baby brother out of his crib.

"Hello there!" she cooed, holding her arms out to him.

Shloimy gurgled in response, treating her to a big smile. When Shifra lifted him, he snuggled against her shoulder. *At least Shloimy still likes me, even if I can't dance.*

By the next day, her mind was made up.

"Mrs. Boxman, can you put me in props instead of dance?" Shifra asked.

Mrs. Boxman lifted a questioning eyebrow. "You want to drop out of dance?"

Well, I would love to dance, Shifra wanted to say, *but I can't do it without messing up everything. That's why I'm quitting.*

Instead Shifra simply shook her head, lifting big, sad brown eyes to gaze into her teacher's friendly blue ones.

Mrs. Boxman reluctantly switched Shifra into the props group. Shifra began working on props, but

she felt like a robot. She would move things behind the curtain and organize what was needed before the next scene. Yet when she watched the dancers curtsy, lunge, and fly across the stage, her heart would flutter. She wished that she, too, could be one of them, but then she would hear the girls' words replaying in her mind: *Klutz... You do not know how to dance...*

With a sigh, she went back to get the next prop.

Her mother greeted her when she came home. "Shifra, guess what! Shloimy took his first steps today!"

"Mazel tov, Shloimy!" Shifra kissed the baby's soft cheek. "Let me see you do it!"

Mommy stood Shloimy up, waited for him to balance himself, and stepped away. Grinning proudly, Shloimy toddled four steps toward Shifra's open arms before landing, plop, onto the floor. Shifra watched carefully as Shloimy pulled himself up and took another few steps.

Then he fell again, and her heart dropped. Poor baby! But once again, he lifted himself up and waddled the last few steps straight into Shifra's arms.

"Hurray!" Shifra cheered, smothering him with kisses. "You did it!"

Shloimy tossed his head back, his soft brown curls flowing down his neck, and he beamed.

Suddenly, Shifra realized something. Shloimy fell down a bunch of times, but he didn't quit. He just got right back up and tried again, and...he succeeded!

She ran up to her room and closed the door. She began practicing the dances she had watched the girls doing. At first she kept tripping and messing up, but each time she thought of giving up, Shloimy popped into her mind, and she kept at it. Finally, after a full hour of work, she felt like she was getting better. Panting, she sank onto her bed for a rest.

Maybe, if I practice every day...who knows? Maybe I can try the dance group again?

Every day Shifra spent time in her room, working on the dances. She didn't stop until every step was perfect, but she was scared to try dancing again together with the other girls. What if she got nervous and messed up again? She decided to just play it safe and stick with props.

The day of the performance arrived. Smiling mothers, grandmothers, and sisters poured into the auditorium and took their seats, but behind stage Mrs. Boxman's lips were turned into a worried frown.

"I don't know what to do," she confided to the other teachers. "Tzirel is sick, and I really need a replacement dancer."

Shifra was heaving some flowers across the stage for a garden scene and overheard Mrs. Boxman's comment.

She approached her teacher. "Mrs. Boxman, can I dance in Tzirel's place?"

"You? Can you?" Mrs. Boxman studied Shifra uncertainly.

"Yes," Shifra said confidently. "I practiced almost every night. I know the dances really well now."

"Then go right ahead," Mrs. Boxman said, "and thank you."

After making sure the props were set up correctly, Shifra took her place among the dancers. She flew, circled, and jumped at just the right times and in the right places, her steps in perfect sync with all the others girls. Because she hadn't given up, and so she, too, had become a dancer.

The Turnaround

Warm rays of sunlight poured through Michoel's window, nudging him awake. After a mighty stretch, Michoel felt ready to jump up and get ready for school. Today was the day of their history field trip, and he was excited to go. The history center gave tours of homes from two hundred years ago, showing how people used to live in the olden days. There would be butter churning and pottery making and all different types of crafts to try, plus a real farm to walk through.

Then, as if a hammer had knocked him on the head, Michoel remembered something, or rather, someone, namely Zevy Braun. He'd be coming on the trip, too. Suddenly, Michoel didn't want to go anymore.

From the minute Zevy Braun had entered Michoel's class, things had been going steadily downhill for Michoel. He could never guess why, but right from the start, Zevy seemed to have something against him.

"Hey, dummy," Zevy would taunt him, "how are you today?"

If Michoel raised his hand in class to answer a question, as soon as the teacher's back was turned, his words would be greeted by snickering or eye-rolling from Zevy. When Michoel wanted to join a game during recess, Zevy would make comments like, "Why pick the slowpoke?"

Michoel used to like school, but now he felt like a punctured balloon. Like a pin, Zevy had managed to push all of the air out of him, leaving him feeling flat and dull.

"Michoel?" Mommy came in to make sure he was awake. "Today's your big trip. Rise and shine, so you'll be ready on time!"

Michoel let out a groan. "I don't feel well, Mommy. I think I need to stay home."

"What's the matter?" Mommy leaned over him, looking concerned, and placed a hand on his forehead.

"My throat hurts," Michoel whimpered in a weak-sounding voice. "My stomach, too."

"Hmm," Mommy answered, cocking her head to the side. "Why don't you rest a little longer, and then we'll see how you're doing?"

"Great!" Michoel agreed, burrowing under his covers and closing his eyes.

After a few minutes, Michoel grew restless. He washed, *davened*, and felt his stomach start to rumble. If Mommy saw him eating breakfast and looking healthy, she would take him to school! So he sighed, reached for a book, and lay back down.

The hours ticked slowly by, and Michoel imagined all the fun his friends must be having on the trip. It wasn't fair that Zevy had taken that away from him, but at least he was safe at home, away from all the nastiness that made his fists clench and his stomach tie itself in knots. Mommy gave him some pretzels, soup, and toast; and she even played a few games with him. Still the day seemed like it was lasting forever.

When Mommy woke Michoel the next morning, he tried to convince her that he wasn't well enough to go back to school yet.

"Michoel," Mommy said firmly, "you seem fine. I want you to go to school today."

With heavy feet and an even heavier heart, Michoel got ready and boarded the bus on time.

"Hey, dummy, we missed you yesterday!" Zevy's voice greeted him loud and clear, and Michoel turned his face to the window and stared at the passing cars.

After recess Michoel came back inside the classroom, only to find his books strewn all over the floor. At lunchtime Zevy stuck his foot out just when Michoel was passing by, and in a flash, Michoel found himself sprawled flat on the floor.

Should I tell Rebbi? Michoel wondered, dusting himself off. *But if Zevy gets in trouble, he'll just be even angrier at me. He'll probably keep doing nasty things to me when Rebbi is not around. Maybe I should switch schools...*

After lunch when the boys were back in their seats, Rebbi began teaching *parshah*. "This week's *parshah* talks about the meeting between Yaakov and Eisav..."

Rebbi's voice grew softer and sounded like it was coming from far away, and Michoel found himself peering out from behind a sand dune. His eyes grew wide when he saw a holy-looking man gathering a huge amount of animals.

"Send these to my brother as a gift," he told his servant.

Why, that's Yaakov Avinu! Michoel realized, his heart thumping excitedly.

While Michoel stared, Yaakov separated his family into two groups, talking to them in soothing tones. Finally, Yaakov closed his eyes and *davened*.

Michoel had never watched someone *daven* with such feeling, and he could hardly tear his eyes away. He could almost see the words flying like birds, rushing higher and higher toward Shamayim. Surely the *malachim* were rushing around with great joy, busily collecting the *tefillos* and bringing them straight to Hashem...

Michoel blinked, and the picture disappeared. He looked around and saw Rebbi still standing in front of the class, teaching, while he and his classmates sat in their regular seats.

I've got it! Michoel punched his palm with his other hand, and a smile curved his lips. *I know just what I need to do in order to deal with Zevy Braun.*

Michoel called Zevy after school. He was shaking from his head to his toes, but he was determined to try his plan. "Hey, Zevy, my grandparents bought me a Gameboy for my birthday. It's a lot of fun. Would you like to come over and try it out?"

Holding his breath, Michoel waited anxiously to hear what Zevy would answer. Would he yell something mean and slam the phone down?

"Uh, sure," Zevy said. "I'll be over in a few minutes."

Michoel nearly whooped with joy. Soon after, there was a knock at the door. Michoel opened it and allowed Zevy to step inside.

"Want some cookies?" he offered, steering Zevy toward the kitchen. "My mother just made these."

A few pleasant hours passed, with the boys munching and playing games together.

"Well, thanks," Zevy finally said, getting up to go. "See you tomorrow."

That night, Michoel stared up at his ceiling, listening to the owls hooting and the cicadas chirping.

"Hashem," he whispered, "I need Your help. I want things to get better between me and Zevy. I'll do my best, but it's really all up to You." He said a *perek* of Tehillim, followed by Shema. Feeling like he had done his part, he drifted into a comforting sleep.

The next day Zevy wasn't in school.

"Who can bring Zevy the work he missed?" Rebbi's eyes swept the room.

"I will," Michoel volunteered, once again remembering the gift Yaakov had sent to calm Eisav's boiling anger.

"Thanks," Zevy said when Michoel showed up at his door that afternoon holding the packet of work he had missed. "I wasn't feeling well earlier in the day, but I'm a lot better now. I should be back in school tomorrow."

"That's good," Michoel replied. "See you." With a wave, he started down the walkway leading away from Zevy's house.

"Um, Michoel!" Zevy called out after him.

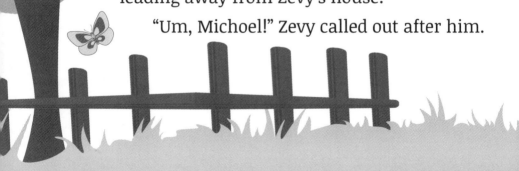

Michoel turned around, a question mark in his eyes.

"Do you want to stay and shoot some hoops?"

"Sure!" Michoel grinned. "I'll cream you!"

"We'll see about that," Zevy replied, an answering grin lighting up his eyes.

The next day at school, Michoel's class ran outside the moment the recess bell sounded. Zevy was captain of one team, and Michoel gulped, wondering what was in store for him. Would Zevy go back to treating him meanly? Had all his efforts been for nothing?

"I'll take Michoel," Zevy announced. Grinning widely, Michoel made his way over to stand next to Zevy.

The score doesn't really matter, Michoel thought, taking his position in the field. *I've already won something much more important.*

And as the ball zoomed toward him, Michoel swung his bat and hit a home run.

Avigayil Sprouts Wings

The new mystery book beckoned to Avigayil like a sparkling ocean calling to a sailor. *Maybe I'll just read one chapter*, she decided, *and then I'll do my homework.*

"Hi, Avigayil!" Mommy greeted her cheerfully. "How was school?"

"Great, *baruch Hashem*. I just won a new book from the reading contest, and I can't wait to start it." Avigayil's green eyes glittered with excitement.

"Mazel tov, honey. I'm proud of you. But I wonder if you can hold off on reading and do something else instead."

The smile on Avigayil's face quickly vanished, and her brow puckered. "What?" she asked, her tone disinterested. There was nothing else she wanted more than to go ahead with her plans and sink her teeth into the world of a brand-new story.

"Shifra was up all night with Yitzy, and she's totally exhausted. I thought you could offer to watch Shmuly in the living room while I make supper, so she can take a nap."

Watch Shmuly? Why, that kid didn't stop for a minute! He was a three-year-old dynamo who could empty containers of toys faster than you could say wait! Avigayil's eyes narrowed into angry slits, and she felt like stamping her foot and crying out. Why should her plans be ruined just because her sister had a new baby? Was it her fault that baby Yitzy had kept Shifra up all night? It didn't seem fair, and it was on the tip of her tongue to tell her mother that she simply wasn't available to be a babysitter.

She heard the sound of footsteps coming down the

stairs, and she looked carefully at Shifra who was cradling little Yitzy in her arms. Shifra's eyes had dark circles around them, and her face looked pale.

"Oh, okay," Avigayil agreed, heaving a mighty sigh. "I can watch Shmuly, but not for too long," she added.

"Thanks so much, Avigayil," Shifra murmured gratefully. "I just need to close my eyes a little bit, and you always make Shmuly so happy."

Like a little tornado, Shmuly barreled into the room and began dumping canisters of toys. In seconds the shiny hardwood floors were carpeted by a colorful mixture of blocks and puzzles.

"Wait, Shmuly!" Avigayil said. "Let's build with Magna-Tiles, okay?"

"I'm gonna make a castle," Shmuly said, stacking the tiles as high as they could go.

"That sounds like fun," Avigayil said. "Who lives in the castle?"

"Our family!" Shmuly declared. "There's room for you and Bubby and Zeidy, but there's water all around," he explained, putting blue tiles down in every direction. "We'll need a boat to get in and out."

The minutes ticked by as Shmuly wove his story, and Avigayil found herself fascinated by his creative imagination. *I wonder if he'll be a writer when he grows up*, she mused. While she played with her nephew, she began to enjoy herself. He was really cute, even if he was a little wild sometimes.

When Shifra came back downstairs, her eyes looked a little brighter. "Avigayil, I can't thank you enough," she said warmly. "That power nap was the best medicine. You did a huge mitzvah."

"Glad to help," Avigayil replied, and to her surprise, she really meant it. Her heart soared with the joy of helping someone in need.

●●●

The next time Avigayil was asked to help was on a bright, beautiful Sunday afternoon. Her best friend,

Aviva, had come to her door, wearing her helmet and an eager grin.

"Do you want to ride scooters together?" Aviva asked.

"Sure!" Avigayil exclaimed. "I'll just tell my mother."

"Not so fast," Mommy said, and Avigayil felt her heart plummet, like a heavy stone tossed into the middle of a lake and sinking fast. "I was going to ask if you could go down to Zeidy's room and spend an hour with him. I have to go shopping, and he could really use the company."

Zeidy had just come to stay with her family after being in the hospital. He was feeling much better, but sometimes he got lonely and just wanted someone to talk to. But why, Avigayil wondered angrily, did that someone have to be her? Especially now, when she wanted to go out and have some fun! It wasn't fair.

"Do I have to?" she wanted to know, meeting Mommy's gaze.

"Do you have to?" Mommy echoed, and Avigayil heard the disappointment in her mother's voice. "I guess you don't have to," Mommy said softly. "But…"

"Great!" Avigayil shouted and flew out the door to join Aviva. "See you later!" she called, fastening her helmet and grabbing her scooter.

As she and Aviva rode their scooters up and down the block, a fresh breeze blowing into their faces, Avigayil tried to figure out what was bothering her. Somehow she wasn't having as much fun as usual, and she didn't understand why. Even when she and Aviva raced down the last hill of the block and she won, she didn't feel that usual lift of excitement.

Suddenly she knew why. A picture of Zeidy filled her mind. Her gentle, loving Zeidy who always took her out for ice cream and special treats. Zeidy, who loved to push her on the swings and watch her zoom down the slides in the park. Zeidy, who patiently taught her to ride a two-wheeler, and enjoyed helping her with her schoolwork. Now it was *her* turn to give to him, and she had failed.

"Ready for round two?" Aviva asked.

"Actually, I can't," Avigayil said. "I have to go back home now. Maybe tomorrow?"

"Is everything okay?" Aviva wanted to know, her eyebrows knitted together in puzzlement.

"It will be," Avigayil replied determinedly, revving up her pace and gliding home as fast as possible.

"Hi, Zeidy, how are you feeling?" she asked, racing into his room.

"Better now that you're here," he replied, his blue eyes crinkling up at the edges. A bubble of contentment swelled inside Avigayil as she pulled a chair up close to his rocking chair.

•••

"Avigayil, I've got a surprise for you!" Mommy greeted her one afternoon after school. "Tante Chanie and Uncle Yaakov are going away for a short vacation, and they'll be passing through our city on their way. Guess where they'll be dropping your cousin Shevy off?!"

Eyes glittering with excitement, Avigayil clapped her hands together and crowed, "Yes! Shevy's coming to our house! We haven't seen each other in ages!" Then she asked, "How long will she be staying?"

Mommy laughed and said, "Thursday, Friday, Shabbos, and Sunday. How does that sound?"

"Like a dream," Avigayil answered. "I have to go make some welcome signs!" And off she dashed to find her markers and paper so she could welcome Shevy in grand style.

It felt like forever until Thursday arrived, but finally the day came, and her cousin Shevy walked into her house.

"Hi, Shevy!" Avigayil called, feeling that if her smile grew any wider, her face would split in two.

"Hi, Avigayil!" Shevy gave her an answering grin.

"Come on up to my room!" Avigayil invited. "Let's

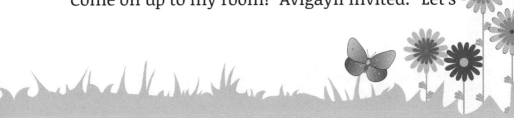

put your stuff down, and then we can go jump on the trampoline."

"Trampoline?" Shevy repeated. "Okay, I guess."

"It will be a blast, you'll see," Avigayil assured her.

Avigayil jumped, did cartwheels, and laughed, while Shevy just watched, a small smile playing on her lips.

"Come on, Shevy, why aren't you jumping?"

Shevy shrugged and folded her arms across her chest. "Can we go inside now?" she asked.

"But we just started!" Avigayil protested. "Can we hold hands and jump together?"

"I guess," Shevy agreed, and the two girls bobbed up and down.

"Avigayil..." Shevy wheezed after a few minutes. "I had enough. Please, let's go in."

"Oh, okay," Avigayil said, disappointed. Then she brightened. "Hey, I know what we can do now! Let's play Step-It-Up!" Avigayil raced ahead, motioning Shevy to follow her. "What level are you on?"

Once again, after a few minutes, Shevy looked winded.

"Don't you have any board games?" she asked.

"Board games?" Avigayil echoed. "Why would you want to play board games?"

Pursing her lips together, Shevy turned her face away and blinked back tears.

"So, are you having fun?" Avigayil asked Shevy that night, when they were both lying in bed, tucked under their covers. "Maybe we can go biking tomorrow before Shabbos!" she added as an afterthought.

"Um, I guess," Shevy murmured, but her voice sounded muffled.

"Shevy," Avigayil said, propping her head up so she could face her cousin. "Is something wrong?"

Shevy sighed. "I guess I'm not really a running-jumping kind of person. I like playing games and drawing—that kind of thing."

"But that's so bor—" Avigayil clamped her hand over her mouth before allowing the word to escape. She didn't want to insult Shevy, but why didn't Shevy like doing exciting things?

An owl hooted, and Avigayil pictured it perched up on a tree branch, fluffing its wings and staring all around. Then a funny thought popped into her mind, and she imagined taking away the owl's wings. How would it get around? she wondered. Or what if it were forced to stay awake in the daytime and go to sleep at night? The poor owl would be all mixed up. It would not be a very happy bird.

Just as the owl gave another loud hoot, Avigayil was suddenly struck by a realization: The same way an owl needs its wings and its time at night to do what it's supposed to do, so each person needs her own things and her own way to feel right and be who she's supposed to be. Everyone is different, and what's right for one of us isn't always right for the other. She needed to understand that...and to understand Shevy's needs and wants.

"You know what, Shevy?" Avigayil whispered. "I have this great art set with markers and crayons and stamps. If there's time tomorrow, do you want to try it out?"

"I would love that!" Shevy agreed, and Avigayil could hear the eagerness in her cousin's voice.

"Great!" Avigayil said warmly, and soon she drifted off into the world of dreams.

●●●

"I had a great time," Shevy said when it was time for her to leave on Sunday. "Thanks for everything, Avigayil."

Avigayil glanced at the Monopoly game they had just finished and then back to her cousin's satisfied expression. "I had fun, too," she replied. "Thanks so much for coming."

She went outside to get her scooter and see if Aviva was available. As the breeze brushed past her, and the trees and flowers waved

their heads in greeting, Avigayil felt on top of the world. It was that feeling again, the one that came when she thought of another person's needs and not just her own. Picking up her pace, Avigayil rode her scooter down the block, feeling like she had just sprouted wings.

A Tale of Two Brothers

cicles hung from roofs and tree branches, standing strong against the gusts of chilly wind. While the weather was freezing outside, the temperature inside Eli and Noach's room felt almost as cold. That's what happens when two brothers are not on speaking terms. Backs turned, the twins both went about their business, ignoring each other. If their eyes happened to meet at any time, it was hard to tell whose glare was frostier.

Eli buried his nose in his book, trying to read, but the words refused to stick in his head. Because Eli was angry, and when he was angry, it was hard for him to concentrate.

I can't believe he did that! Eli fumed. *That was a brand-new CD that I just got for my birthday. How dare Noach take it without permission! And if that wasn't bad enough, he took it to Pinny's house and lost it! I won't forgive him! Next time he wants to borrow something, I won't let. Maybe I should take something of his and lose it, "by mistake," of course. It would serve him right!*

Noach's thoughts were just as angry. *Eli is making such a big deal out of a little CD! I told him I was sorry. I even told him that next time I get some money, I'll buy him a new CD, but no, that wasn't good enough. He had to scream and yell at me. Well, if that's the way Mr. Perfect wants to be, then he can stay that way—by himself. When he wants to play a game or do something with me, I'll just be too busy.*

The temperature stayed in the freezing zone for the next few days. People bundled up in hats, scarves, coats, and gloves just to walk to their cars, and no one stayed outside for an extra minute. But

the Zemel household was definitely not the place to go if someone wanted to warm up with friendly smiles and good cheer. Because the silent war between Eli and Noach was still going strong.

One evening, Eli was passing by Tatty's study when he overheard Tatty's voice. It sounded very stern.

"Noach," Tatty was saying, "that's the fifth time in just a few weeks that your teachers have called to complain about your behavior. If I get one more call about something like this, you're grounded, and yes, I know Pinny is having his birthday party this Sunday. It's your choice. If you want to go, you know what you have to do."

Eli could picture Noach hanging his head, a sad look in his eyes, and his heart twisted. Eli knew Noach didn't usually mean to make trouble; he just liked to have fun, and sometimes things got out of control... Hey, wait a minute, why was he feeling bad for Noach? Noach

deserved to be punished! For a minute Eli had forgotten their fight.

In a flash, like a light bulb flicking on in a dark room, everything came flooding back, and Eli found himself hoping that Noach would do one more thing wrong and get punished. *That will serve Noach right!*

The next day in school, Rabbi Shapiro was in the middle of teaching *parshah*. He turned to the board and began writing something. With a sudden swish, a paper airplane zoomed overhead, coming in for a landing right on top of Rebbi's shoulder. Rabbi Shapiro whirled around, his face red.

"Who's responsible for this?" Rabbi Shapiro asked in a low voice, and his gaze swept the class.

Looking around, Eli wondered who had such chutzpah. The instant his eyes locked with Noach's, he knew. Staring at his twin brother, Eli saw his fear-filled gaze, and he understood: Noach hadn't done it on purpose. Once again, he had just been playing, and his airplane had simply veered off course. Rebbi probably wouldn't believe him. After all, Noach had already gotten into trouble several times that week, for things that *hadn't* been mistakes.

He is my brother, Eli mused. *My twin brother and I feel bad for him. He really is trying hard not to get into any more trouble... He'll be so sad if he has to miss his best friend's birthday party, all because of a little mistake...*

"I'm really sorry, Rebbi," Eli heard himself say. He could feel twenty pairs of eyes boring into him, but he swallowed and looked straight ahead. "It was a mistake."

All the boys held their breath, waiting for Rebbi's reaction. Rebbi peered at Eli, and his eyes softened.

"That was brave of you to admit your mistake," Rebbi said. "Thank you for the apology, and make sure it doesn't happen again."

Noach flashed Eli a look of pure gratitude. Eli winked and looked away.

At recess Noach ran over to Eli. "You saved my life!" he said. "Thank you, thank you, thank you!"

That night, Eli's soft snoring filled the bedroom, but Noach couldn't fall asleep. Something was bothering him.

It's not fair that Eli should take the blame for something I did. I need to tell the truth. I need to speak to Rebbi about what really happened, even if it means I'll get grounded.

The next morning, when Noach told Eli that he was going to tell Rebbi the real story, Eli was flabbergasted.

"But—but why? Do you want to get grounded and miss Pinny's party?"

"No," Noach said, "I really don't. But this just doesn't feel right. I need to be honest, so I'm going to tell Rebbi."

As the two boys went downstairs for

breakfast, Eli snuck a look at his brother. *He may be a troublemaker*, Eli mused, *but he's a great guy.*

After class that day, Noach approached Rabbi Shapiro. His hands were clammy and cold, and the closer he came to Rebbi's desk, the more he wanted to run far away in the opposite direction.

"Yes, Noach? Can I help you?"

"I-I just wanted to tell Rebbi w-what happened yesterday," Noach began. "About the paper airplane..."

Rebbi's eyebrows lifted while he listened to the story.

"I am really impressed," he said warmly, placing a hand on Noach's shoulder. "It must have been very hard for you to tell me the *emes*, but you did it anyway. *Yasher koach*, Noach."

"Am I—am I in trouble?" Noach squeaked.

"Not today," Rebbi replied with a smile. "You told me it wasn't on purpose, and I believe you. Just make sure not to play with paper airplanes in class, and

then these things won't happen by mistake, either."

"Yippee!" Noach shouted. "Thanks, Rebbi!" And he dashed off to tell his brother Eli the good news.

All Aboard to Fairville!

"It's not fair!" Libby's mouth was turned down in an angry scowl. "Why did Meir get the last cookie? I wanted it!"

"It doesn't feel fair, does it?" Mommy gazed into Libby's narrowed eyes. "But does life always have to be fair?"

"Yes!" Libby stamped her foot. "Everyone should get the same stuff—always."

It happened again when Libby was playing Checkers with her older sister, Chumi.

"Why do you always win?" she protested, folding her arms across her chest and refusing to help clean up the game. "It's not fair!"

"Does life always have to be fair?" Chumi asked, repeating her mother's earlier question.

"Yes," Libby insisted. "If you win twice, then I should win twice. If you get a treat, so should I. Why shouldn't everything be equal?"

Shrugging her shoulders, Chumi put the game away. "Life just isn't that way," she said, heading for the kitchen. "Maybe you'll understand when you're older."

Never! Libby thought. *It's just plain wrong when people are treated differently. If everyone would always get the same things, I'm sure people would be a lot happier.*

"What did you get on your Chumash test?" Esti, Libby's best friend, asked her the next day in school.

"An eighty," Libby replied. "How about you?"

"I got a hundred," Esti shared, a proud smile lighting up her face.

Sniffing, Libby turned away. *Not fair! Why*

does Esti always get better marks than me? I studied, too!

That night, Libby lay in bed thinking. *When I'm a mother,* she decided, *all my kids will be treated equally. I'll be the fairest person ever.* With that thought in mind, she slipped right into a dream.

"Welcome aboard!" a stewardess called, motioning to her to come forward. "Step into this plane, and we will take you to the best place in the world!"

Curious and excited, Libby entered the little plane. Before she knew it, its doors had closed behind her, and they were soaring higher and higher, dipping through the white, puffy clouds in the clear blue sky.

"Would you care for a drink?" the stewardess asked.

"That would be great," Libby said. "I'll take Sprite."

"All we have is root beer," the stewardess said. "Root beer is the pilot's favorite drink, and in the interest of fairness, every passenger is given the same thing."

Root beer? Libby thought. *Yuck!* But she didn't want to seem rude, so she simply said, "No, thank you. Do you have water?"

"I'm sorry, dear," the stewardess said, shaking her head. "Just root beer."

"I'll pass, thank you," Libby declared stiffly, turning to peer out the window and wondering when they would arrive.

"Prepare for landing," the pilot announced and in a flash, they glided smoothly to the ground.

"Welcome to the city of Fairville!" the pilot said. "Enjoy your stay, and thank you for flying Justice Airlines."

This is the most beautiful place I've ever seen! Libby thought, her eyes shining. Palm trees waved their greetings, and flowers of all colors and sizes dotted the thick, dark green grass. Blue lakes shimmered and rippled in a gentle breeze, bordered by clean, white sand. Seagulls dipped and soared near the water.

Libby was delighted. Lifting her feet, she ran over to some children who were seated around a picnic table. All the kids were wearing birthday hats.

"Whose birthday is it?" Libby asked a little girl.

"Everyone's," the girl replied in a flat voice.

"Everyone's?" Libby echoed, raising her eyebrows. "How can that be?"

"Simple," the girl continued, sounding robot-like. "In the city of Fairville, all the children celebrate their birthday on the same day and in the same way. So since today's the first day of June, the exact middle point of the year, the mayor of Fairville declared that it is the best day to have a party and wish everyone a happy birthday."

A perfectly square hunk of chocolate cake topped with a scoop of butter pecan ice cream was set in front of Libby, and Libby saw that all the children were receiving the same portion.

Libby's heart fell. Butter pecan ice cream always made her nauseous. She turned to the waitress who had just served her. "Excuse me, but is there any other flavor of ice cream?"

"No, there isn't," the waitress replied crisply, giving Libby a stern look. "This is Fairville. Everyone is treated the same, or it wouldn't be—"

"Fair," Libby finished the sentence, a sad tone in her voice. "I know," she sighed.

Half-heartedly, she lifted her spoon, made a *brachah*, and began eating the cake.

Another woman appeared, dressed in the exact same white shirt and blue jumper as the waitress. "Now for the presents," she announced.

Each child received a box wrapped in blue and gold wrapping paper, topped with a white bow. Libby eagerly unwrapped the gift and withdrew a brown stuffed bear.

I really wanted a new pair of earrings for my birthday, Libby thought, rubbing her hands over the bear's soft fur. *I already have so many stuffed animals. I don't really play with them much anymore.* Looking

around, she saw every child holding his new toy, the same brown stuffed bear. Some children seemed happy, but others had a glassy look in their eyes, as if they didn't care one way or the other.

I'd like to go see what the rest of this place is like, Libby decided, getting up from the table.

"Thank you," she called to the women in charge, and quickly walked away.

A cobblestone path caught her eye, and she began to follow it. At the end of the path stood a two-story building.

"Fairville School," she read, and walked through the double glass doors.

"Where is the first grade class?" Libby asked the secretary in the office.

"Oh, all of the children learn together, dear," the secretary told her, "in one large classroom. Go straight down the hall until you can't go any further."

Libby tiptoed into class and found a seat at the back of the room.

"Today we will have a test in geography," Mrs. Tzedek announced, passing out the test papers.

Libby raised her hand and waited until the teacher called on her. "I've only just come in," Libby explained, "so I won't be able to take the test. I never learned the material."

"Of course you will take the test," Mrs. Tzedek countered, a stern look in her eye. "In Fairville everyone does the same work, at the same time. Those are the rules of our fair city."

A large tear dripped down Libby's cheek, followed by another in fast pursuit. It wasn't fair! She was going to fail for sure! Sure enough, when she looked over the questions on the test, she couldn't fill in even one answer.

When the recess bell rang, Libby sighed with relief and slipped out of the school building. After walking for a while, she noticed a flight of steps at the side of the road. *Wonder what's up there*, she mused, and skipped up the steps to explore.

A door faced her, with a big sign on it: *Fairville Clothing Store.*

"Why not look around?" she asked herself out loud, entering the large, air-conditioned store.

Libby's eyes bulged when she saw rows and rows of clothing hanging on the racks. Every single piece of clothing looked the exact same: the same color, the same size, the same style—the SAME EVERYTHING! Each skirt was blue, with gold stitching. Each shirt was blue and white, with gold stitching. The coats were winter green, with large black buttons. The sweaters were dusty brown, with tan zippers...

"Excuse me." Libby approached a saleslady, who was wearing the same outfit that hung from every rack in the store. "Do you have clothes in size eight?"

"This," the saleslady said, making a sweeping motion with her hand, "is one size fits all." Chuckling, she added, "You must be new here. Everyone in Fairville wears the same clothes and makes due with the same size. It's only—"

"Fair," Libby gasped in a choked voice, zooming out of the store as fast as her legs could carry her.

"Please," she begged the stewardess when she arrived, panting, at the airport. "Get me on a plane and take me home—FAST!"

Birdsong woke Libby in the morning, and when she opened her eyes, she grinned when she saw her own bedroom walls staring at her.

"Good morning, Libby," Mommy greeted her. "Did you sleep well?"

"Yes, I did," Libby replied. "And I'm sure glad to be home."

Mommy looked at Libby questioningly, but Libby just grinned and began getting ready for school.

"Who knows the answer to the first homework question?" Morah Lesser asked, looking around at all of her students.

Libby and Chani raised their hands at the same time.

"Chani?" Morah Lesser nodded.

Not fair! was Libby's first thought. *I knew the answer, too!* Then she remembered Fairville, and a different thought crossed her mind.

Maybe not everything has to be fair. This time Chani has the chance to answer, and I'll have my turn a different time. Each person gets what she needs, at the right time.

"Libby, can you help me with my books?" Chavie asked when it was time to move to a different classroom. With a broken leg, Chavie was having a hard time getting around, even with her crutches.

"Sure," Libby said, taking Chavie's backpack. She wondered, if one person got hurt in Fairville, did that mean *everyone* had to get hurt, too? Then who would be left to help out, if everyone was hurt at the same time?!

During lunch she sat quietly, studying her friends as she ate. Her eyes rested on each classmate in turn. Shira had a pretty voice, and Leah was a talented

artist. Chedva was good at sports, and she, Libby, did well in school. Chayli was a whiz when it came to math, and Rivka was a great actress. Each person had something special, a gift from Hashem. How was that fair? Each one of them was different in her own way...

"Hi, Libby," Mommy greeted her when she came home. "I had a really busy day today and could use your help getting supper ready. Would you mind making the salad, please, and setting the table?"

It's not fair! The three words were poised on Libby's lips, ready to burst out. Why did Mommy have to give her extra work? Why couldn't Mommy ask her brother and sister to help, too? Then the chores would be evenly divided.

Suddenly Libby remembered a beautiful place with palm trees, lush green grass, and brightly colored flowers, and all her arguments instantly disappeared.

She quietly went to the refrigerator and

began taking out the vegetables. And in her mind's eye, she waved goodbye to that beautiful but awful city called Fairville.

Going Home

One beautiful summer day, when the sun beamed down from a bright blue sky, Mrs. Mann and her daughter got ready for an outing at a nearby park.

"Here's your snack, Chavie." Mommy handed her a bag filled with popcorn, one of her favorite foods, and they began the short walk together.

"Thanks, Ma," Chavie said, holding the bag happily as she skipped along beside her mother.

When they arrived at the park, Chavie dashed toward the swings, leaving her popcorn on a green bench beneath a tall, leafy tree.

"I'm flying!" Chavie called, pumping her legs with all of her strength as she lifted herself higher and higher, feeling as if she were touching the clouds.

When she finished swinging, Chavie climbed up to the tall slide, whooshing down it so fast it took her breath away. After a while, her stomach started rumbling, so she ran to the bench to get her snack.

"My popcorn!" Chavie cried out. "Who took my popcorn? I'm so hungry!"

She whirled around, hoping to catch the popcorn thief. Could it be the brown-haired little boy holding tight as the merry-go-round swung him in circles? Or maybe it was the red-haired girl with the cute dimples making sand castles in the sandbox? Neither one was holding her bag. They weren't even chewing. So where could her snack have gone?

Chavie put her hands on her hips, determined to track down her missing popcorn. She walked all around the park, looking in every possible spot.

When she was all tired out from walking, and was about to give up her search, she spotted a piece of something yellow and fluffy at the far edge of the grassy playing field. Why, it looked like popcorn! She walked another few feet and saw another kernel, but just then a loud squawk startled her.

"Oh!" she said, staring right into the eyes of a large goose. She looked down—and suddenly began to laugh. "Mommy! Come look!" Chavie called.

Her mother came over. "Is something wrong, Chavie?" she asked.

"Look!" Chavie pointed at the goose, her green eyes sparkling with excitement. For there, right beside the goose, was her bag of popcorn, overturned and empty.

"That's my popcorn thief!" Chavie giggled.

"I guess she was hungry," Mommy said, joining in the laughter. The goose honked its agreement, opened its beak, and snapped up a stray piece of popcorn that had landed on the side of its nest.

"Would you like to go closer?" Mommy asked Chavie.

Chavie nodded. She clutched Mommy's hand tightly as together they walked toward the large goose. Mrs. Goose was comfortably settled on a large, brown circular nest, and her black beady eyes met their curious stares. Fluttering her wings, she repositioned herself, and Chavie drew back.

"It's okay," Mommy soothed. "She's not going anywhere. She has to take care of her babies."

"She has babies?" Chavie wondered aloud. "Where are they?"

"Well, she probably has some eggs under her. She has to keep them warm until they hatch."

"I can't wait to see her babies!" Chavie said, jumping with excitement. Tilting her head to the side while looking thoughtfully at Mrs. Goose, Chavie added, "I think I'll call her Popcorn."

Popcorn honked, and Mommy and Chavie shared a smile.

"I think she likes her new name," Mommy said.

Every day Chavie begged her mother to take her to the park so they could check on Popcorn; and every day they found the goose in the same position, wings at her side, sitting comfortably on her nest as she stared into the distance.

"When will the eggs hatch already?" Chavie felt impatient. "I want to see how many babies she'll have."

"Should be any day now," Mommy assured her. "Then you can wish her a big mazel tov."

Chavie nodded and ran toward the swings. She wondered who could fly higher, she on the swing, or Popcorn with her wings. Wouldn't it be amazing if they could fly together... And she closed her eyes and swung faster and faster, higher and higher, above the tallest trees and into the clear blue sky.

A loud honk got her attention, and she opened her eyes in a hurry. What she saw made her face grow hot, and she slowed the swing and jumped

off. Popcorn was waddling around the playground as fast as she could go, while a group of children chased after her, delighting in their game of real "Duck, Duck, Goose." The children laughed and ran faster, and Popcorn stayed just ahead of them, flapping her wings and running her feathery best.

Chavie's eyes flashed with anger, and she stepped right in the path of the racing group of children.

"You stop that right now!" she demanded. "This goose is a mother. She has to sit on her eggs and take care of them, and you're not letting her! How can you be so mean?"

Surprised, the children looked at each other and then at the goose.

"We don't want to hurt her," one boy answered. "We were just having some fun."

"Go play tag with each other," Chavie said. "Can't you see you're scaring her?"

"Aw," one boy complained. "We were having such a good time."

"Come on, guys," another boy said. "She might be right; that goose does look scared. Let's go climb that tree over there instead."

"Oh, okay," the others agreed, reluctantly leaving Popcorn and following their friend.

Chavie stood near Popcorn and waited until they had walked off. Popcorn was important to her, and she wanted those babies to be born strong and healthy.

"It's okay now," Chavie whispered, and Popcorn gazed at her as if she understood.

Popcorn stood still for a few moments, as if to make sure the coast was clear, and then she flapped her wings and let out a honk. She flew upward, and Chavie hoped she was on her way back to her nest.

"Come, Chavie, it's time to go now," her mother called.

"Can we check on Popcorn first? Please, Mommy. Some boys were chasing her, while you were over there by the bench, and I want to make sure she's back where she belongs."

To her relief, they found Popcorn sitting comfortably on top of her nest.

"*Baruch Hashem,*" Chavie breathed.

On their way home, she told her mother how she had rescued Popcorn from the kids who had been chasing her.

"That was nice of you," Mommy said, and Chavie squeezed her mother's hand. Maybe tomorrow, thanks to her intervention, there would be baby goslings to hold! Now that would be fun!

Weeks passed, but there were still no baby goslings. The weather felt heavy and hot, like there was sadness in the air. It was close to Tishah B'Av.

"I know Tishah B'Av is a sad day," Chavie said to her mother as they walked home from the park together one day. "I know we're supposed to cry since we don't have the Beis Hamikdash anymore. But I don't really understand. I never saw the Beis Hamikdash. It's hard to feel sad for something I lost but never had."

Mommy tried to explain. "When we had the Beis Hamikdash," she began, "we were very close to Hashem. He showed us lots of miracles, and we were able to be better Jews because we saw so much *kedushah*. Whenever we did something wrong, we could bring a *korban* and do *teshuvah*—and then Hashem would forgive us. You know that special feeling you get when you tell me 'I'm sorry' for something you did wrong, and I give you a big hug? That's the way it was after we brought a *korban*. We felt clean and fresh, like Hashem forgave us and wrapped us in a big, warm hug.

"Now that we don't have the Beis Hamikdash, everything is so much harder. As much as Hashem still loves us, it's like He's further away. Imagine if Tatty and I lived in one place, and you moved to the other side of the world. We would always love you, of course, but it would be sad to live so far from you."

Chavie thought about that. Yes, it would be sad not to see her parents very often.

"What else happened in the Beis Hamikdash, Mommy?"

"Well," said Mommy, "the *kohanim* would teach us Torah, and they knew so much! When we learned from them, we also grew closer to Hashem. The Beis Hamikdash had very special *keilim* in it. There was the golden Menorah, and the middle flame always stayed lit. The *kohanim* lit the rest of the flames at the beginning of every day. While the *leviim* worked, they sang beautiful songs of Tehillim, to thank Hashem for His kindness. The challah on the golden *Shulchan* stayed warm from week to week. And even though there was so much meat waiting to go on the *Mizbei'ach*, there were never any flies buzzing around. A visit to the Beis Hamikdash meant going to the most special place in the whole world!"

"Wow, Mommy," Chavie said. "I wish I could go..."

Mommy smiled sadly. "That's what Tishah B'Av is for, my dear, to *daven* to Hashem, to help us fix up our mistakes. We hope that soon we won't have to fast anymore, because we'll be able to go to the Beis Hamikdash in Yerushalayim, whenever we want to…"

●●●

"Mommy, I know you're fasting, but do you think…"

It was late on Tishah B'Av afternoon, and her mother looked tired.

"Let me guess—you want to check on Popcorn, the goose?" her mother asked, and Chavie nodded.

"Come." Mommy put out her hand, and they walked to the park slowly together.

"Mommy, look!" Chavie pointed to the nest, and she and Mommy peered inside. The large brown nest was empty. There was no trace of Popcorn or her eggs. Where had they gone? Chavie and her mother looked all around, but there was not a goose or gosling in sight.

"I really wanted to see the babies," Chavie said, disappointed.

"I know you did." Mommy squeezed her hand as they walked across the street. "So did I. I guess they moved somewhere else."

"That empty nest makes me feel so sad," Chavie said. "No mother, no babies. It was such a happy place, and now there's nothing there."

"Chavie, maybe now you can understand Tishah B'Av a little better. Hashem is also sad when His home is empty. The Beis Hamikdash was His house. Can you picture Hashem looking down from Shamayim at His house, and everyone's gone? Where are His children?"

"That is sad, Mommy. So why doesn't He build a new house and bring His children back there?"

Mommy smiled and wiped a tear from her eye. "One day, sweetie. One day soon, *im yirtzeh Hashem*, Mashiach will come, the

Beis Hamikdash will be rebuilt, and we'll all be together in Yerushalayim."

Summer came to an end, and the trees were dressed in red, orange, and gold. One windy afternoon, when the brightly colored leaves danced and fluttered in the cool breeze, Mommy and Chavie were on their way home from school.

"Mommy, why are the cars just sitting here? Why aren't they moving?"

"There's a lot of traffic, honey. I don't know what's causing it."

Sounds of tooting horns filled the air. It seemed that Chavie and her mother weren't the only ones anxious to get home.

"Oh, so that's what's going on!" Mommy said with a laugh. "Look, Chavie!"

Chavie looked out her window, and what she saw made her gasp. Two large geese strutted slowly across the busy street, with a flock of six baby goslings following behind.

A small smile played on Chavie's lips, growing larger and wider as she watched the goose parade. "Mommy, do you think that's Popcorn?" she asked, not wanting to tear her eyes away from the magical sight. "It looks just like her."

"Maybe." Mommy grinned as the geese continued their slow but steady waddle across the street. They appeared not to care about the loud horn-blowing concert.

"Mommy, do you think..." Chavie began.

"Do I think what, Chavie?"

"Well, if Mr. and Mrs. Goose are going home with their babies, and they're all together like a family should be, do you think Mashiach is on his way? Will we also be going back to our real home in Yerushalayim soon?"

"It can happen any day, Chavie. We keep *davening* and hoping that one day soon, our *tefillos* will be answered."

Chavie looked into Mommy's eyes and smiled.

They watched as the last goose stepped onto the sidewalk, and at last, the cars started to move again.

They were going home.